Tanya

For Paul and Alison

This book is a presentation of
Weekly Reader Children's Book Club.

Weekly Reader Children's Book Club
offers book clubs for children from
preschool through junior high school.
For further information write to:
Weekly Reader Children's Book Club
4343 Equity Drive
Columbus, Ohio 43228

Library of Congress Cataloging in Publication Data
Rusling, Albert.
The mouse and Mrs. Proudfoot.
Summary: Mrs. Proudfoot and her daughter Miranda
enjoy their pretty new cottage in the country except
for a resident mouse. They bring in an enormous
number of animals to rout it, with surprising results.
1. Children's-stories, English.[1. Animals —
Fiction. 2. Counting] I. Title. II. Title: Mouse
and Mrs. Proudfoot.
PZ7.R8985Mo 1984   [E]   84-17871
ISBN 0-13-604265-1

Weekly Reader Children's Book Club presents

The Mouse & Mrs. Proudfoot

Albert Rusling

Prentice-Hall, Inc.
Englewood Cliffs
New Jersey

On the top of Cedar Hill, near Squirrel Wood, stood Bluebell Cottage. It was the prettiest cottage in all of Dinglebury.

It had a yellow thatched roof. Pink and red roses covered its white walls, and its windows overlooked a neatly fenced garden full of flowers of every color.

Mrs. Proudfoot and her daughter, Miranda, had recently bought the cottage and had just moved in. But though they didn't know it, there was already someone living in Bluebell Cottage.

"A mouse!" squealed Mrs. Proudfoot, as she and Miranda jumped on to the nearest chair. And indeed there was a mouse – looking up at them from the middle of the carpet – a small, white mouse with a brown patch over one eye and one brown leg.

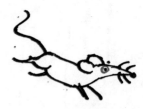

"It will have to go!" said Mrs. Proudfoot. "Hurry to Squirrel Wood, Miranda, and bring back two large owls to chase the mouse away."

Miranda ran to Squirrel Wood and brought back the two largest owls she could find with long, sharp talons and round, dinner-plate eyes. That very day the small, white mouse with a brown patch over one eye and one brown leg was chased away.

All that night the two large owls hooted. They hooted and hooted and hooted. They hooted so loudly that neither Mrs. Proudfoot nor Miranda could sleep a wink.

The next morning Mrs. Proudfoot was very cross.

"They will have to go!" cried Mrs. Proudfoot. "Hurry to the barn, Miranda, and bring back three fat cats to chase the owls away."

Miranda hurried to the barn and chose the three fattest cats she could see. Soon the three fat cats had chased the two large owls with long, sharp talons and round, dinner-plate eyes away.

All the next day the three cats slept in Mrs. Proudfoot's favorite chair. They slept and slept and slept. Mrs. Proudfoot was unable to sit in her favorite chair all day.

That evening she was very cross.

"They will have to go!" gasped Mrs. Proudfoot. "Hurry to the meadow, Miranda, and bring back four sly foxes to chase the fat cats away."

Miranda hurried to the meadow and caught the four slyest foxes she could find with long, bushy tails and pointed ears.

The four sly foxes soon chased the three fat cats off Mrs. Proudfoot's favorite chair and out the door. And that night the four sly foxes ate all the chocolate cakes Mrs. Proudfoot had made for the village fair They ate and ate and ate.

The next day Mrs. Proudfoot was very cross.

"They will have to go!" wailed Mrs. Proudfoot. "Hurry to the farm, Miranda, and bring back five lively dogs to chase the sly foxes away."

Farmer Hacket gave Miranda five of his liveliest dogs — two long sausage dogs, two large, shaggy sheep dogs, and one small, spotty dog with a black button nose.

The five dogs quickly chased the four sly foxes out of the cottage and into the fields.

All that night the five lively dogs chewed the legs of Mrs. Proudfoot's oak dining table. They chewed and chewed and chewed.

The next morning Mrs. Proudfoot was very cross.

"They will have to go!" groaned Mrs. Proudfoot. "Hurry to the forest, Miranda, and bring back six wild boars to chase the lively dogs away."

Miranda ran to the forest and brought back the six wildest boars she could catch. Before they knew it the six wild boars had chased the five dogs – two thin sausage dogs, two large, shaggy sheep dogs and the small spotty dog with the black button nose – out of the cottage window.

All that day the six wild boars charged around the cottage. They charged around and around and around until a large hole was worn in Mrs. Proudfoot's carpet.

That night Mrs. Proudfoot was very cross.

"They will have to go!" sobbed Mrs. Proudfoot. "Hurry to the forester's hut, Miranda, and bring back seven hunters to chase the wild boars away."

Miranda hurried to the forester's hut to find seven hunters. When the seven hunters arrived at the cottage they shot off their guns and shouted loudly and the six wild boars ran out the door and across the meadow.

All that day the hunters sat in Mrs. Proudfoot's kitchen and drank her home-made elderberry juice. They drank and drank and drank until all the bottles were empty.

That evening Mrs. Proudfoot was very cross.

"They will have to go!" croaked Mrs. Proudfoot. "Hurry to the caves, Miranda, and bring back eight ferocious grizzly bears to chase the hunters away."

Miranda did as she was asked and chose the eight most ferocious grizzly bears she could find. As soon as the grizzly bears entered the cottage the seven hunters climbed up the chimney and ran off across the cornfields.

All that night the grizzly bears licked the honey from Mrs. Proudfoot's jars of honey. They licked and licked and licked until there was no honey left for breakfast.

The next morning Mrs. Proudfoot was very cross.

"They will have to go!" shrieked Mrs. Proudfoot. "Hurry to the zoo, Miranda, and bring back nine brave lions to chase the grizzly bears away."

Miranda ran to the zoo and chose the nine largest, bravest lions she could find. As the lions approached the cottage they roared and snarled angrily. Even before they reached the garden the eight ferocious grizzly bears started running as fast as they could through the kitchen door.

All day long the lions roared. They roared and roared and roared until all Mrs. Proudfoot's crockery had fallen off the shelf and broken on the floor.

That night Mrs. Proudfoot was very cross.

"They will have to go!" howled Mrs. Proudfoot. "Hurry to the circus, Miranda, and bring back ten enormous elephants to chase the lions away."

Miranda, exhausted by this time, reached the circus and collected the ten most enormous elephants she could find. When the nine brave lions saw the elephants they fled in terror.

Unfortunately the elephants were so vast that once they were inside the cottage there was no room for anyone else. Mrs. Proudfoot and Miranda had to sleep in the garden.

The next day Mrs. Proudfoot was very cross.

"They will have to go!" screamed Mrs. Proudfoot. "Hurry into the fields, Miranda, and bring back a mouse to chase the elephants away."

So Miranda hurried into the field and returned with a mouse – a small, white mouse with a brown patch over one eye and one brown leg. Soon the elephants had fled, and all that day Mrs. Proudfoot, Miranda and the small, white mouse sat in front of the open fire eating toasted muffins.

Mrs. Proudfoot was very happy.